# Pirates Can Pay Attention

Tom Easton

**WINDMILL BOOKS**
New York

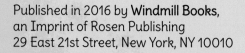

Published in 2016 by **Windmill Books,**
an Imprint of Rosen Publishing
29 East 21st Street, New York, NY 10010

Commissioning editor: Victoria Brooker
Creative design: Basement68
Illustrations© Mike Gordon

Manufactured in
the United States of America

CPSIA Compliance Information: Batch #BW16PK:
For Further Information contact Rosen Publishing,
New York, New York at 1-800-237-9932

Cataloging-in-Publication Data

Easton, Tom.
Pirates can pay attention / by Tom Easton.
p. cm. — (Pirate pals)
Includes index.
ISBN 978-1-5081-9152-0 (pbk.)
ISBN 978-1-5081-9153-7 (6-pack)
ISBN 978-1-5081-9163-6 (library binding)
1. Listening — Juvenile fiction. I. Easton,
Tom (Children's fiction writer). II. Title.
PZ7.E13159 Pir 2016
[F]—d23

# Pirates Can Pay Attention

Written by
**Tom Easton**

Illustrated by
**Mike Gordon**

**WINDMILL**
BOOKS ™

New York

The crew of the *Golden Duck* was very excited. They were in Port Pegleg and their pockets were bulging with treasure.

"Now listen carefully," Captain Cod told the pirates. "Watch out for my old enemy, Captain Blackears, and his Horrid Pirates. I saw their ship, the *Bad Dog*, moored on the other side of the harbor."

But no one was listening to the captain as
he spoke. "Remember, keep your treasure
well hidden," he said. "Otherwise
the Horrid Pirates will steal it."

"Polly, you look after the ship,"
the Captain said. But Polly wasn't paying
attention either. She had seen a big sign
in town which read "Cracker Factory."

As soon as the gangplank was in place, the pirates rushed off into the town. Sam and Nell headed for the shops. Davy and Pete headed for the ice cream parlor. And Polly? Well, Polly wanted a cracker to eat.

"What about this dress?"
Nell said, showing Sam
one with skulls and
crossbones on it.

"It's really expensive!" Sam said,
his eyes bulging at the price tag.
Nell shrugged. "That's OK. I have loads
of treasure," she said, slapping a big bag
of gold coins on the counter.

At the ice cream parlor, Davy and Pete had just ordered the biggest ice cream sundaes in the shop.

Pete was staring at a pirate captain sitting at a table. The Captain's ears were as black as tar.

"I haven't seen you lads in here before," the pirate captain said.

"We just arrived this morning," Pete said.

"On the *Golden Duck*."

"That's Captain Cod's ship, isn't it?" the captain asked, rubbing one of his ears.

"Yes," replied Davy, with his mouth full of ice cream. "Why do you ask?"

Meanwhile, poor Polly Parrot had been disappointed to find the factory made the wrong sort of crackers.

The exploding kind.
She sat on the weather vane on top of the town hall and went to sleep.

Captain Cod had been shopping. He'd bought
a new peg leg and an enormous hat.
He wandered back to the ship, humming
a shanty. On the way, he had to hide in
an alley as two Horrid Pirates ran out of
a dress shop, each carrying a bag of gold.

More Horrid Pirates came rushing
out of the ice cream parlor.

"Stop, thief!" someone called.
Captain Cod crawled past
so they wouldn't see him.

No one was at the
ship when the Captain
returned.

He grumbled and looked
at his watch.

Polly Parrot woke with a start as a group of cackling Horrid Pirates clattered along the street below.

"Let's get this treasure back to the *Bad Dog*," said Captain Blackears.

Polly squawked in alarm and flapped her way back to the ship.

"Calm down, Polly" said Captain Cod when she arrived. "Tell me everything that's happened."
So Polly did. The captain listened very carefully.

Four pirates trudged back to the *Golden Duck*.
 "I wish the Captain had told us about
the Horrid Pirates," Pete said.
 "I wish he'd told us to keep quiet
        about the treasure," Nell added.
 "I'm hungry," Davy said.

The Captain was waiting for them back at the ship. All the pirates started shouting at once.

"They took our gold," Nell said.

"What are we going to do?" Sam pleaded.

"Why didn't you tell us about the Horrid Pirates?" Pete demanded.

"Is there any food?" Davy asked.

"LISTEN!" the Captain shouted.
Everyone stopped talking.
"The reason you're in this mess
is that you didn't listen to me."

There was a flapping sound overhead.
"Polly!" they all cried. The parrot dropped
a package on the deck. Nell unwrapped it.

"Crackers!" she said.

"Great," said Davy. "I'm starving."

"Not those sort of crackers," Nell said.

"These are the exploding kind."

"Polly and I know exactly where the stolen treasure is," the Captain said, a glint in his eye. "And we know exactly how we're going to get it back." He told them the plan and, this time, the crew listened.

That night, when all the good folk of Port Pegleg were safely tucked in their beds, the quiet was broken by a CRACK and a BANG and a POP and a BOOM down at the harbor.

The Horrid Pirates woke up alarmed and rushed down the gangplank to investigate the noise. They didn't notice, in the confusion, that the *Golden Duck* had slipped quietly along the other side of their ship.

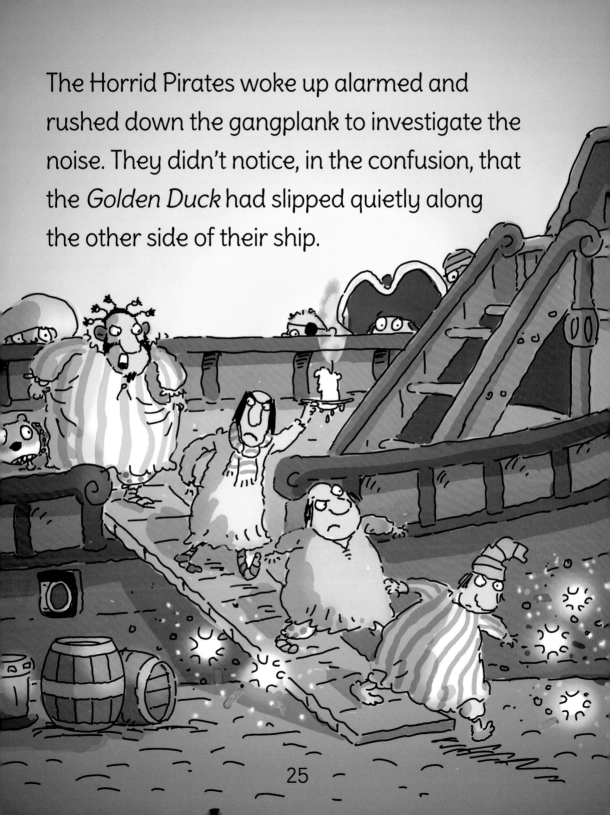

"Now!" whispered the Captain.
They leapt aboard the *Bad Dog*
and snatched the treasure bags.

"Hey!" roared Captain Blackears, as he saw what was happening. "I"ll get you, Cod!"

But the Horrid Pirates were too late. Captain Cod's crew sprang back on board the *Golden Duck* and cast off. They sailed out of the harbor, the Horrid Pirates shouting rude names after them.

"What are they shouting?" Sam asked.
The Captain clapped his hands over Sam's
ears and said, "Maybe this one time it's
better NOT to listen."

# NOTES FOR PARENTS AND TEACHERS

## Pirate Pals

The books in the *Pirate Pals* series are designed to help children recognize the virtues of good manners and behavior. Reading these books will show children that their actions have a real effect on people around them, helping them to recognize what is right and wrong, and to think about what to do when faced with difficult choices.

## Pirates Can Pay Attention

*Pirates Can Pay Attention* is intended to be an engaging and enjoyable read for children aged 4-7. The book will help them recognize why it's important to listen and pay attention.

When Captain Cod gives the pirates advice on how to behave on shore, he is trying to keep them safe. Unfortunately, the pirates allow themselves to be distracted by thoughts of the fun that awaits them. After they lose their gold, they complain that the captain didn't warn them of the dangers. To make matters worse, they interrupt the captain when he's trying to help them. In contrast, when he learns of his crew's predicament, the captain listens carefully to Polly to get the information he needs to form a plan. By distracting the Horrid Pirates with too much noise the captain saves the day.

Learning to listen is a vital skill used in all areas of life. Children need to be able to listen carefully in order to successfully complete tasks and keep safe at school, at home and out and about. Being able to listen effectively will help them learn good manners as well as how to interact with others – skills that don't come naturally to all children. Listening is a social skill and enables communication and exchanging of ideas.

It's difficult for children to remember to listen. Especially when there are so many distractions. We are all surrounded by sounds and sights and learning to focus on the important things can take time. Help them to listen carefully.

Active listening requires people to learn to judge when to speak and when to remain silent. It is a vital aspect of any team-based activity. Without listening we cannot make sense of, assess, or respond to what we hear.

Remember to listen to children and make a show of it. They imitate behavior and if you don't show you are listening, then they will not consider listening to be important.

## Suggested follow-up activities

Talk about the events in the book. Ask children to identify the times when the pirates didn't listen, and when they did.

Play listening games. Fill a bag with objects that make a distinctive sound and ask them to guess what each one is.

Read out loud regularly to children so they become used to the rhythms and patterns of your voice. Change the names in a familiar story and ask them to identify what was different.

Make eye contact with them when you give advice or instruction. Get down to the child's level to make sure you have their full attention.

Listing things aids memory. Play memory games, such as "I went to the shop and bought an apple..."

# BOOKS TO SHARE

*Everybody Matters: A First Look at Respect* by Pat Thomas and Lesley Harker (Wayland, 2014)

Everyone deserves respect, whether it is by being treated fairly or by not being discriminated against because they are different. This book shows how you can earn respect by being polite, honest, or listening to others.

*Monkey Needs to Listen (Behavior Matters)* by Sue Graves (Watts, 2011)

Monkey is so excited about a go-kart race that he doesn't listen to any of the instructions. He doesn't stop to check his kart and he nearly ruins the race for all the animals. Can Monkey learn to listen and pay attention or will the race be abandoned for good?

*The Worst Day of My Life Ever: My Story about Listening and Following Instructions* by Julia Cook

RJ has a bad day. He's late, gets into trouble for not handing in homework, and makes a mess at home. With his mom's help, he learns that his problems are happening because he's not listening. This story shows how listening can turn bad days into good days.